North Dakota

Minnesota

South Dakota

Wisconsin

Maine

apshire

Massachusetts

New York

Rhode Island

Connecticut

Michigan

Pennsylvania

New Jersey

Iowa

Nebraska

Ohio

Illinois

Indiana

Delaware

Maryland

Washington, D.C.

West Virginia

Virginia

Kansas

Missouri

Kentucky

North Carolina

Tennessee

Oklahoma

South Carolina

Arkansas

Georgia

Mississippi

Alabama

Texas

Louisiana

Florida

The Twelve Days of Christmas in Georgia

written by
Susan Rosson Spain

illustrated by
Elizabeth O. Dulemba

STERLING
New York / London

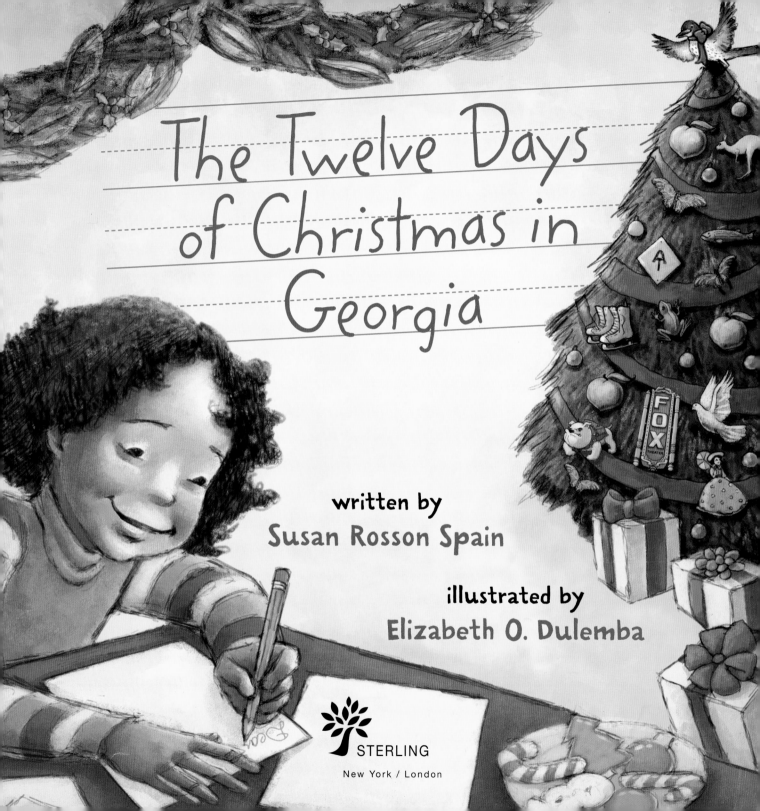

Dear Jacob,

Merry Christmas from the Peach State! I didn't mail your presents yet because GUESS WHAT? Mom, Dad, and I want you to come and get them yourself!

You won't believe how much there is to do here. Georgia's not just peaches, peanuts, and possums, you know. You might see anything, from bears in the mountains to alligators in the swamps. We're going to visit lots of fun places all over the state during the holidays, and we can't wait for you to get here so we can get started.

So how about it, cousin? Christmas in Dixie will be one to remember! See you soon!

Your cousin,
Ava

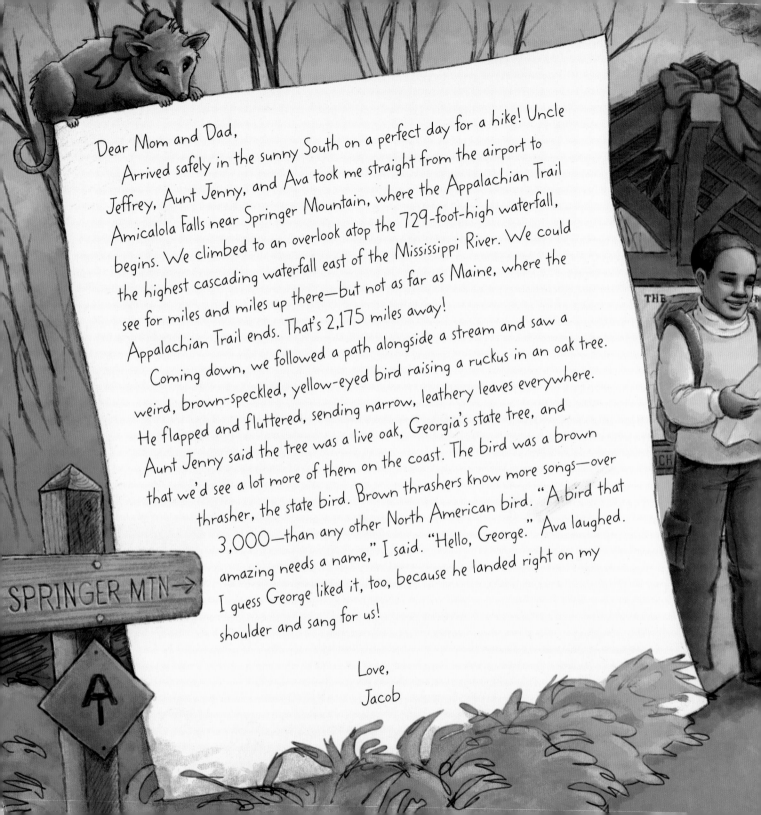

Dear Mom and Dad,

Arrived safely in the sunny South on a perfect day for a hike! Uncle Jeffrey, Aunt Jenny, and Ava took me straight from the airport to Amicalola Falls near Springer Mountain, where the Appalachian Trail begins. We climbed to an overlook atop the 729-foot-high waterfall, the highest cascading waterfall east of the Mississippi River. We could see for miles and miles up there—but not as far as Maine, where the Appalachian Trail ends. That's 2,175 miles away!

Coming down, we followed a path alongside a stream and saw a weird, brown-speckled, yellow-eyed bird raising a ruckus in an oak tree. He flapped and fluttered, sending narrow, leathery leaves everywhere. Aunt Jenny said the tree was a live oak, Georgia's state tree, and that we'd see a lot more of them on the coast. The bird was a brown thrasher, the state bird. Brown thrashers know more songs—over 3,000—than any other North American bird. "A bird that amazing needs a name," I said. "Hello, George." Ava laughed. I guess George liked it, too, because he landed right on my shoulder and sang for us!

Love,
Jacob

SPRINGER MTN →

AT

On the first day of Christmas,
my cousin gave to me . . .

a thrasher
in a live oak tree.

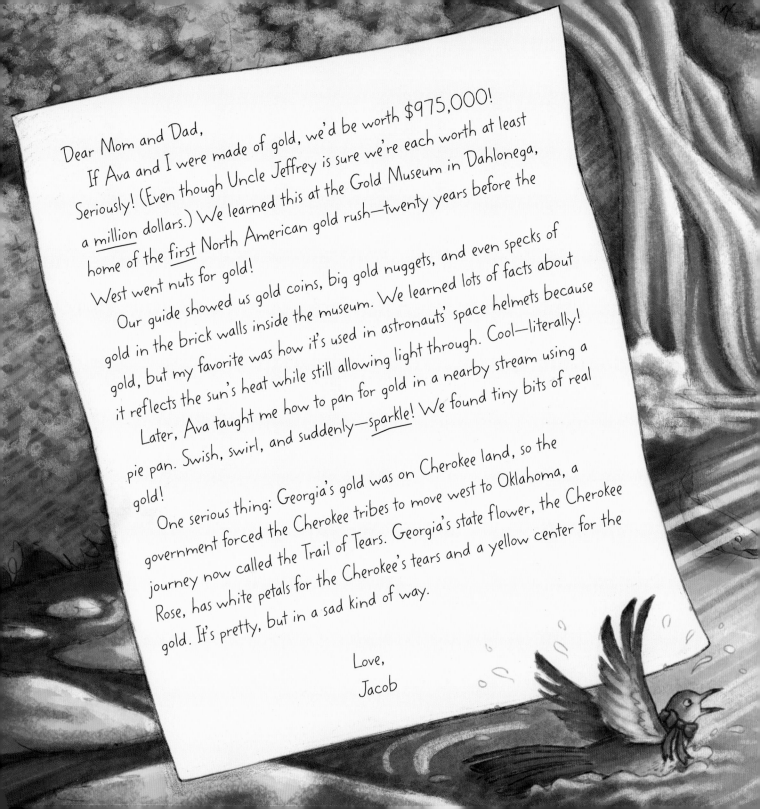

Dear Mom and Dad,

If Ava and I were made of gold, we'd be worth $975,000! Seriously! (Even though Uncle Jeffrey is sure we're each worth at least a _million_ dollars.) We learned this at the Gold Museum in Dahlonega, home of the _first_ North American gold rush—twenty years before the West went nuts for gold!

Our guide showed us gold coins, big gold nuggets, and even specks of gold in the brick walls inside the museum. We learned lots of facts about gold, but my favorite was how it's used in astronauts' space helmets because it reflects the sun's heat while still allowing light through. Cool—literally!

Later, Ava taught me how to pan for gold in a nearby stream using a pie pan. Swish, swirl, and suddenly—_sparkle_! We found tiny bits of real gold!

One serious thing: Georgia's gold was on Cherokee land, so the government forced the Cherokee tribes to move west to Oklahoma, a journey now called the Trail of Tears. Georgia's state flower, the Cherokee Rose, has white petals for the Cherokee's tears and a yellow center for the gold. It's pretty, but in a sad kind of way.

Love,
Jacob

Dear Mom and Dad,

Can you imagine dangling from a rope 400 feet from the ground while carving men on horseback into the side of a granite mountain? Me neither until today, when we visited Stone Mountain and I saw the <u>huge</u> carving for myself. The memorial to Confederate President Jefferson Davis and Generals Robert E. Lee and Thomas J. "Stonewall" Jackson took more than 50 years to complete and is the biggest stone sculpture of its kind in the world. In fact, General Lee's horse, Traveller, is so long, you could park a school bus on his rump. Whoa, Nellie! We rode the tram to the top of the mountain and could see the whole Atlanta skyline.

Ava says maybe I could visit again in the summer, when there's an amazing rock-and-roll laser light show projected right on the carving. Hundreds of people bring blankets to the Memorial Hall lawn to watch and sing along with the music. The three horsemen magically "come alive" and gallop off the mountain, then return in the patriotic grand finale with fireworks exploding high above them. Awesome!

Riding off into the sunset,
Jacob

Dear Mom and Dad,

I have a dream! And even though my dream is to be an astronaut, I will never think of those words the same way again after today's visit to the Martin Luther King Jr. National Historic Site in Atlanta.

Ava and I took a tour of Dr. King's boyhood home, then walked through the Children of Courage exhibit. Wow. Before the Civil Rights Movement, life was way different than it is today for African-American kids. Ava's granddad wasn't allowed to go to the same schools as white kids or even drink from the same water fountains. But Dr. King worked for equality and peaceful change, and because of that, dreams are starting to come true for people of all colors.

Next, the most perfect thing happened. You know how doves are symbols of peace? Well, just as we left the exhibit, four doves flew right over our heads! I'll bet they knew it was Dr. King's neighborhood!

At the Visitor's Center, Ava and I got a fun activity book. When we finish the pages in it, we'll be official Junior Park Rangers. How cool is that?

Peace,
Jacob

On the fourth day of Christmas,
my cousin gave to me . . .

A cooing doves

3 horsemen, 2 pans of gold,
and a thrasher in a live oak tree.

Dear Mom and Dad,

Ava says the lakes and ponds in Georgia never freeze over, but we went ice-skating outdoors anyway—at the artificially cooled ice rink at Centennial Olympic Park. The park was built for the 1996 Olympic Games in Atlanta, the 100th anniversary of the modern Olympic Games. Round and round we skated, singing Christmas songs under all those twinkling lights. Being there made me feel like I could win a medal, too!

Afterward we drank hot chocolate and explored the walkways and courtyard near the park's ringed fountains, searching the engraved bricks for the one Uncle Jeffrey and Aunt Jenny "bought" to help fund the '96 Games. Uncle Jeffrey gave us a clue where to look, otherwise we might never have found it—there are over 686,000 engraved bricks! As the sun set, the ringed fountains shot water high into the sky, lit from behind with colorful lights. Ava says that in the summer, kids and joggers splash in the fountains to cool off. What fun!

Love,
Jacob

On the fifth day of Christmas,
my cousin gave to me . . .

5 Olympic rings

4 cooing doves, 3 horsemen, 2 pans of gold,
and a thrasher in a live oak tree.

Dear Mom and Dad,

I laughed so hard today my stomach is sore! At the Center for Puppetry Arts we watched a crazy puppet show. And it wasn't just funny; it was amazing. Ava and I could hardly believe the puppets weren't moving on their own! We had to look really hard to see the puppeteers, covered head-to-toe in black clothing, swooping and waving behind the stage.

The exhibits were filled with famous puppets. "Ernie!" I shouted, just about the same time Ava yelled, "Look! It's the Swedish Chef!" Aunt Jenny and Uncle Jeffrey cracked up over a hog named Dr. Strangepork (what a name!) from "Pigs in Space." We all ran into old friends today made by Jim Henson, probably the most famous puppeteer ever!

In the Center's Create-A-Puppet Workshop, Ava and I joined other kids in inventing some wacky new friends of our own. You'll never guess what my puppet is, but I'll give you a hint: George is very confused!

Tonight we're going to ring in the New Year by watching the giant Georgia Peach drop exactly at midnight. Ten, nine, eight, seven, six, five, four, three, two, one . . .

HAPPY NEW YEAR!
Jacob

Dear Mom and Dad,

Since we were up so late ringing in the New Year, I napped almost all the way to Tybee Island this morning. I might've slept even longer if Ava hadn't started picking confetti out of my hair. (Ouch!) Once we got inside the Marine Science Center, though, I perked right up. We saw baby alligators, strange polka-dot batfish, and striped burrfish—all water creatures native to Georgia. There was a whole room just for turtles, too, plus a touchtank with a bunch of crabs you could pick up!

My favorite thing was learning about the right whale, Georgia's state marine mammal. The tour guide told us that right whales are baleens, which means they don't have teeth—they filter food out of the water through a tough fringed band that hangs from their upper jaw. Weird! Scientists are pretty sure the Georgia/North Florida coast is the only place right whales go to calve. Every winter, pregnant whales swim from the North Atlantic to these warmer coastal waters. Just think—maybe a right whale is being born out there this very minute! Happy birthday, little whale!

Afterward we went out on the pavilion pier to look for dolphins. We spotted <u>seven</u> of them!

Splish-splash,
Jacob

On the seventh day of Christmas,
my cousin gave to me . . .

7 dolphins swimming

6 puppets playing, 5 Olympic rings,
4 cooing doves, 3 horsemen, 2 pans of gold,
and a thrasher in a live oak tree.

Dear Mom and Dad,

We went <u>wild</u> today—at the Okefenokee National Wildlife Refuge! Okefenokee is a Choctaw word meaning "trembling earth." If you stomp on an unstable layer of peat here, sometimes nearby bushes shake. Yikes!

On a boat tour we spotted turtles, otters, and even an alligator. Our guide said alligators are lazy this time of year. I'll bet the otters were glad. Alligators <u>eat</u> otters! The guide also showed us three "little green monsters"—that's what he called the carnivorous plants. Pitcher plants, butterworts, and sundews trap flies and other insects for food. (Me, I'd rather have a Georgia peach!)

The birds in the refuge were noisy—herons, red cockaded woodpeckers (they're endangered), and long-legged sandhill cranes— plus about 230 other bird species. Loudest of all, though, were the frogs. Pig frogs, leopard frogs, green tree frogs (Georgia's state amphibian), cricket frogs, and chorus frogs all croaked in a funky swamp song. Later, Ava and I had a contest to see who could make a sound just like the pig frog. I won—I sounded exactly like a pig!

Your swamp-creature son,
Jacob

Dear Mom and Dad,

Today we visited Habitat for Humanity's Global Village and Discovery Center in Americus, just 10 miles from Plains, where President Jimmy Carter used to grow peanuts. Habitat for Humanity's goal is to build houses for people who desperately need them—not just poor people in the United States, but all over the world. And President Carter is Habitat's most famous volunteer!

It's hard to believe, but having a house isn't a normal thing for millions of kids. In the Village, Ava and I explored 15 kinds of houses Habitat builds in other countries. Did you know that in India, windows have to have bars on them to keep out roaming monkeys? And houses in Papua, New Guinea, are built on stilts to keep them dry! Ava and I helped our guide pull the lever on a press that shapes earth-and-cement "bricks," just like the ones they use to build houses in Africa. Very cool.

Later we ate sandwiches (Georgia peanut butter and Georgia peach jam, of course!) in an African schoolhouse. It was just a roof over some benches, with a blackboard up front. A school with no walls—can you believe it?

Love,
Jacob

P.S. If we lived in India, I would let the monkeys come inside!

Dear Mom and Dad,

I had insects crawling all over me today. But don't worry—butterflies don't bite!

We got to meet them when we visited the Cecil B. Day Butterfly Center, North America's largest glass-enclosed tropical conservatory, inside Callaway Gardens at Pine Mountain. There were so many butterflies zipping around, the air looked alive! Ava's hair did, too, when they landed on her head!

My favorite part was the Transformation Station, a big glass case where chrysalides hang from cork panels. I remember learning in school about the butterfly's four-stage life cycle—egg, caterpillar, chrysalis, and butterfly—but now I've seen it in action! Some chrysalides were bright yellow or green, others were brown or gray and looked like bark or dead leaves. Ava spotted one of them opening, and about a half hour later, a beautiful yellow, black, and white butterfly sat drying its wings. WOW!

Our guide said the Butterfly Center is helping save acres of rainforest by buying chrysalides from places like Malaysia and Tanzania. If people in those regions were not able to make money by gathering chrysalides, they would have to clear many more valuable rainforest acres to make money farming instead.

Love,
Jacob

Dear Mom and Dad,

We were movin' and groovin' today at the Georgia Music Hall of Fame in Macon!

While Aunt Jenny and Uncle Jeffrey walked the streets of Tune Town exploring exhibits of Hall-of-Famers like R.E.M. and the B-52s, Ava and I headed for the Music Factory, a wing just for kids. We taped our own voices at the Notation Station, and when we played the recording back, WOW, did we rock! Next we performed "Chopsticks" with our feet on a giant keyboard built into the floor, and tried the wall of giant instruments. If we pressed the button matching the instrument we played, we could hear that instrument's part in a song!

Ava says there are fun kids' programs all the time through M.I.K.E.—Music in Kids' Education. During the summer, there's even a Songwriter Camp where professional musicians help kids write their own songs! I'm going to have to come back here soon, okay?

Love,
Jacob

P.S. Is there such a thing as a <u>singing</u> astronaut?

Slap Organ

Dear Mom and Dad,

Did you know you can go "down under" down South? It's true! With about 300 kangaroos, Dawsonville's Kangaroo Conservation Center has the largest mob (group of kangaroos) anywhere outside of Australia! The Center's normal season is March through November, but since the weather was perfect, Uncle Jeffrey called and got special permission for a mid-winter visit!

Dawsonville's climate is a lot like the kangaroo's native Australian climate, and so is the habitat built for the mob, right down to a billabong. (That's a watering hole.) There's a long path they call a walkabout, too, where you can watch the young joeys doing their three favorite things: hopping, scratching, and eating. Adult kangaroos can run—I mean hop—55 miles per hour. That's as fast as a car zooming down the highway! And they can jump the length of a school bus. Crikey!

Another fun thing about visiting the center is that you can learn how to throw a boomerang. Get it right, and it'll come back to you. I think I'll be a boomerang, too, and come right back to Georgia. I miss it already.

G'day, mates!
(Or maybe I should say, "Bye y'all"!)
Jacob

On the twelfth day of Christmas, my cousin gave to me . . .

12 kangas bouncing

11 rockers rocking, **10** butterflies flitting, **9** bricks for stacking,
8 frogs a-croaking, **7** dolphins swimming, **6** puppets playing,
5 Olympic rings, **4** cooing doves, **3** horsemen, **2** pans of gold,
and a thrasher in a live oak tree.

Georgia: The Peach State

Capital: Atlanta · **State abbreviation:** GA · **State bird:** the brown thrasher · **State flower:** the Cherokee rose · **State reptile:** the gopher tortoise · **State butterfly:** the tiger swallowtail **State marine mammal:** the right whale · **State fish:** the largemouth bass · **State song:** "Georgia on My Mind"

Some Famous Georgians:

James Earl "Jimmy" Carter, Jr. (1924–), born in Plains, served as the 39th president of the United States. A novelist, poet, and author of more than twenty books, President Carter is most noted for working to improve the lives of the poor, and for promoting diplomacy over war to settle differences. He won the Nobel Peace Prize in 2002. Carter is a tireless volunteer for Habitat for Humanity.

Ray Charles (1930–2004) was born into severe poverty in Albany. When he was only five years old and just learning to play piano, he began to go blind. By seven, his vision was gone entirely. But RC, as he was called, went on to read and write braille, and mastered not only the piano, but the alto saxophone. He sang everything from rhythm and blues to soul, jazz, country, and pop, becoming a sensation in the world of music. His most famous recordings are "Georgia on My Mind" and "America the Beautiful."

Juliette Gordon Low (1860–1927) was from Savannah. After learning of a boy's scouting program during a trip to England, she returned to Savannah and founded a similar program for girls: the Girl Scouts of America.

Margaret Mitchell (1900–1949), born in Atlanta, wrote *Gone with the Wind*, one of the world's most well-known novels. Published in 1936, it won the Pulitzer Prize for fiction the following year. The motion picture, released in 1939, remains one of the most loved films of all time.

John S. Pemberton (1831–1888), born in Knoxville, was a pharmacist, chemist, and the inventor of Coca-Cola. Pemberton marketed his original formula as a cure for headaches, exhaustion, and to calm nerves.

Jack Roosevelt "Jackie" Robinson (1919–1972), from Cairo, was the first African-American to play Major League baseball in the modern era. He was National League Rookie of the Year in 1947, an All-Star player six years in a row, and National League Most Valuable Player in 1949. His jersey number, #42, is now retired.

Alice Walker (1944–), born to sharecroppers in Eatonton, is a famous novelist, poet, and activist. Her most famous novel, *The Color Purple*, won the Pulitzer Prize in 1983, and was made into both a major motion picture in 1985 and a Broadway play in 2005.

To Jennifer, Rebekah, Rita, and Lauren, my own "Georgia peaches."

Special thanks to Lynda Bryan at the Dahlonega Gold Museum, Faye Walmsley at the Martin Luther King, Jr. National Historic Site, Rachel Crumbley at Callaway Gardens, Maria Procopio at the Tybee Island Marine Science Center, Larry Perrault at Habitat for Humanity's Global Village and Discovery Center, Kate Pika at the Kangaroo Conservation Center, and Jared Wright at the Georgia Music Hall of Fame. All of you helped me enormously.
—S.R.S.

For Stan (always) and all my family living in the each State!
—E.O.D.

Library of Congress Cataloging-in-Publication Data

Spain, Susan Rosson.
The twelve days of Christmas in Georgia / written by Susan Rosson Spain ; illustrated by Elizabeth O. Dulemba.
p. cm.
Summary: Jacob writes a letter home each of the twelve days he spends exploring Georgia at Christmastime, as his cousin Ava shows him everything from a brown thrasher in a live oak tree to twelve bouncing kangaroos. Includes facts about Georgia.
ISBN 978-1-4027-7008-1
1. Georgia—Juvenile fiction. [1. Georgia—Fiction. 2. Christmas—Fiction. 3. Cousins—Fiction. 4. Letters—Fiction.] I. Dulemba, Elizabeth O., ill. II. Title.
PZ7.S73188Twe 2010
[E]—dc22
2009021852

Lot#:
2 4 6 8 10 9 7 5 3 1
06/10

Published by Sterling Publishing Co., Inc.
387 Park Avenue South, New York, NY 10016
Text © 2010 by Susan Rosson Spain
Illustrations © 2010 by Elizabeth O. Dulemba
The original illustrations for this book were created digitally.
Distributed in Canada by Sterling Publishing
c/o Canadian Manda Group, 165 Dufferin Street
Toronto, Ontario, Canada M6K 3H6
Distributed in the United Kingdom by GMC Distribution Services
Castle Place, 166 High Street, Lewes, East Sussex, England BN71XU
Distributed in Australia by Capricorn Link (Australia) Pty. Ltd.
P.O. Box 704, Windsor, NSW 2756, Australia

Printed in China
All rights reserved

Sterling ISBN 978-1-4027-7008-1

For information about custom editions, special sales, premium and corporate purchases,
please contact Sterling Special Sales Department at 800-805-5489 or specialsales@sterlingpublishing.com.

Designed by Kate Moll.

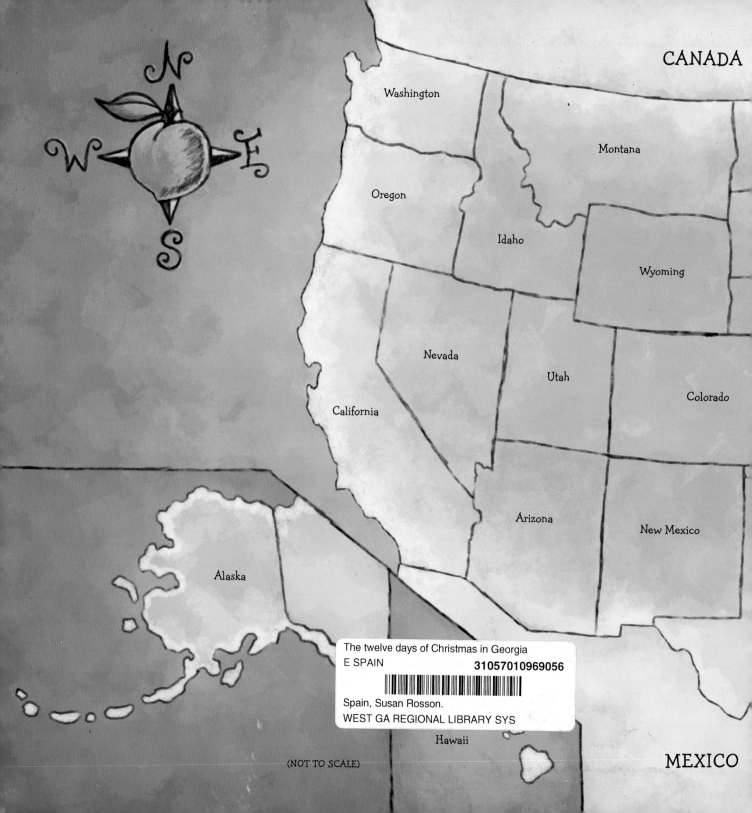

CANADA

Washington

Montana

Oregon

Idaho

Wyoming

Nevada

Utah

Colorado

California

Arizona

New Mexico

Alaska

Hawaii

MEXICO

(NOT TO SCALE)